ALBERT'S
TOOTHACHE

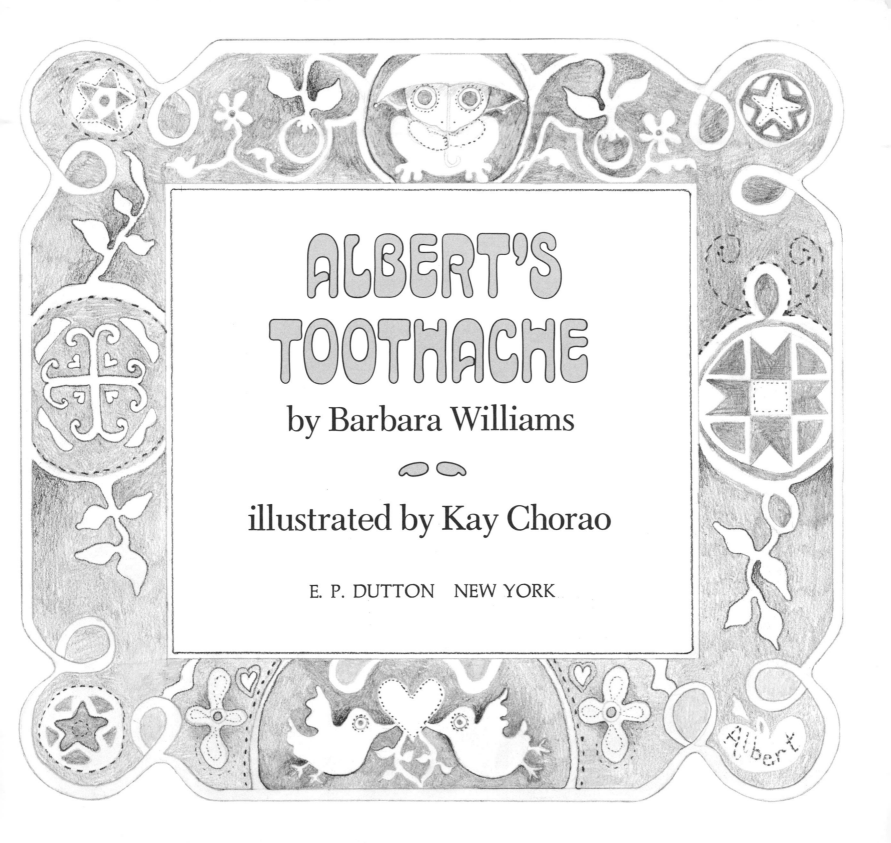

ALBERT'S TOOTHACHE

by Barbara Williams

illustrated by Kay Chorao

E. P. DUTTON   NEW YORK

Unicorn is a registered trademark of E. P. Dutton

Library of Congress number 74-4040
ISBN 0-525-44363-0

Published in the United States by E. P. Dutton,
2 Park Avenue, New York, N.Y. 10016,
a division of NAL Penguin Inc.

Published simultaneously in Canada by
Fitzhenry & Whiteside Limited, Toronto

Editor: Ann Durell   Designer: Riki Levinson

Printed in the U.S.A
First Unicorn Edition 1988   W
10 9 8 7 6 5 4 3 2 1

For Kim

One morning Albert Turtle complained that he had a toothache.

"That's impossible," said his father, pointing to his own toothless mouth. "No one in our family has ever had a toothache."

Just the same, Albert was sure he had a toothache and needed to stay in bed.

"Who's afraid of a toothache?" boasted his brother Homer.

"See," said Albert's father. "Homer doesn't have a toothache. And I don't have a toothache. And Marybelle doesn't have a toothache. And your mother doesn't have a toothache. It is impossible for anyone in our family to have a toothache."

"You never believe me," said Albert.

"I'd believe you if you told the truth," said his father.

"You believed Homer when he said he didn't break the window," Albert reminded his father.

"I'm worried about Albert," said Albert's mother at breakfast.

"You *should* be worried about a boy who doesn't tell the truth," said Albert's father as he left for work.

"Albert just doesn't want to eat his black ants," said Marybelle.

"If I had a toothache, I'd still want to eat my black ants," announced Homer.

"Come eat your black ants, Albert," called his mother.

But Albert just moaned softly from the bedroom.

Albert's mother kissed Homer and Marybelle good-bye and sat down in her worrying chair. She worried and worried.

Then she thought of something. She got up and went to work in the kitchen.

"Look," she said to Albert. "I've fixed you a special breakfast of all your favorite things—rotting oak bark garnished with sunflower seeds, a dried aspen leaf, and half a green caterpillar."

"I can't eat anything," said Albert, poking the tip of his nose out from under the covers. "I have a toothache."

"Of course you don't have a toothache," said his mother.

"You never believe me," said Albert.

"I'd believe you if you told the truth," said Albert's mother.

"You believed Dad when he said he caught a seven-pound trout," complained Albert.

Albert's mother took the tray back to the kitchen
and went outside to her worrying swing on the porch.
She worried and worried.

Then she got a baseball and went into Albert's room.

"Come play catch with me," she said. "You can teach me how to throw a spitball."

"I can't teach you how to throw an old spitball," said Albert. "I have a toothache."

"You just think you have a toothache," said his mother. "Come on, you can play catch if you try."

"You never believe me," whined Albert. "You believed Marybelle when she said she was the only girl in her class who didn't have a pair of black boots with zippers."

Albert's mother put the ball away and went outside to
her worrying rock in the sun. She worried and worried.

Then she got a big book and took it into Albert's room.
"Look, Albert, I brought the family album to show you
the pictures we took in Disneyland. Sit up, Albert."

"I can't sit up," said Albert. "Why don't you ever believe
me?" And a big tear rolled down his cheek.

Albert's mother put the family album away and went into the living room to lie down on her worrying sofa. She worried and worried. She was still worrying when Marybelle and Homer came home.

"How's Albert?" asked Marybelle.

"He still says he has a toothache," said Albert's mother.

"He just didn't want to fight Dilworth Dunlap," explained Marybelle. "Dilworth Dunlap was waiting for him after school."

"If I had a toothache, I'd still fight Dilworth Dunlap," announced Homer.

"Is that son of yours still playing possum?" Albert's father asked when he got home from work.

"Yes," said Albert's mother. "I wish that he would remember he's a turtle."

"He just knew we were having gray spider legs for dinner," said Marybelle.

"I don't want any gray spider legs either," said Homer.

After dinner Grandmother Turtle came over with chewing gum for all the children.

"Can I have Albert's?" asked Marybelle.

"Of course not, it's Albert's," said his grandmother.

"He won't want it. He says he has a toothache," said Marybelle.

"Isn't that terrible?" said Albert's mother.

"Can you believe your grandson would say an impossible thing like that?" asked Albert's father.

"The trouble with all of you is that you never believe him," said Albert's grandmother.

Albert's grandmother went into his bedroom. "Well," she said, "I hear you have a toothache."

"Yes'm," said Albert.

"*Where* do you have a toothache?" asked Albert's grandmother.

"On my left toe," said Albert, sticking his foot out from under the covers. "A gopher bit me when I stepped in his hole."

"Well, I have just the thing to fix a toothache," said Albert's grandmother. She took her handkerchief from her purse and wrapped it around Albert's toe.

Albert smiled toothlessly and got out of bed.